My Friends Make Me HAPPY!

For ET

ISBN 978-1-338-33047-2

12 11 10 9 8 7 6 5 4 3 2   18 19 20 21 22 23

Printed in the U.S.A.   40

First Scholastic printing, October 2018

The illustrations in this book were done digitally.
The text type was set in Chaloops and Eatwell Chubby.
The display type was set in Eatwell Chubby.

My Friends
Make Me
HAPPY!

JAN THOMAS

Yay!
Look who's coming!
My **FRIENDS!**

SCHOLASTIC INC.

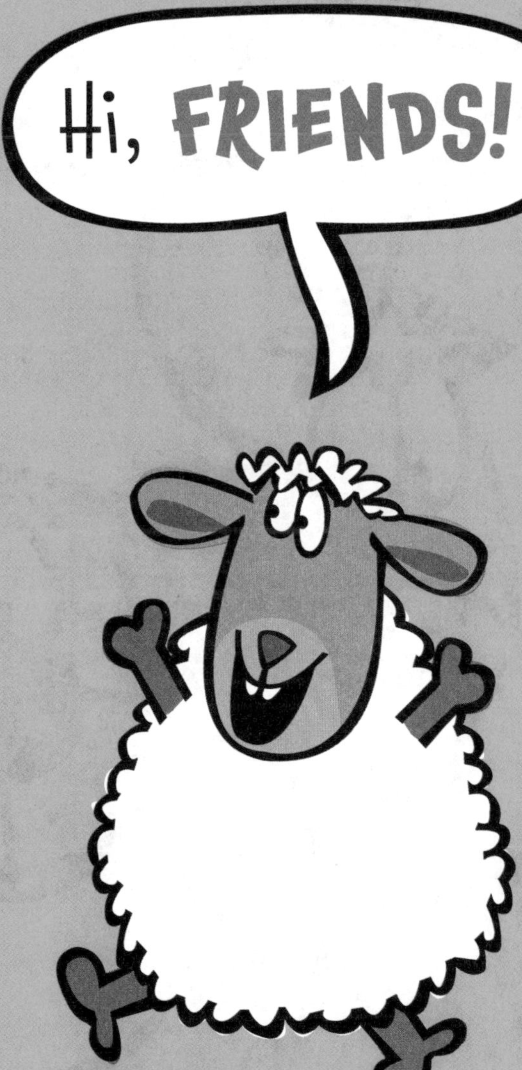
Hi, FRIENDS!

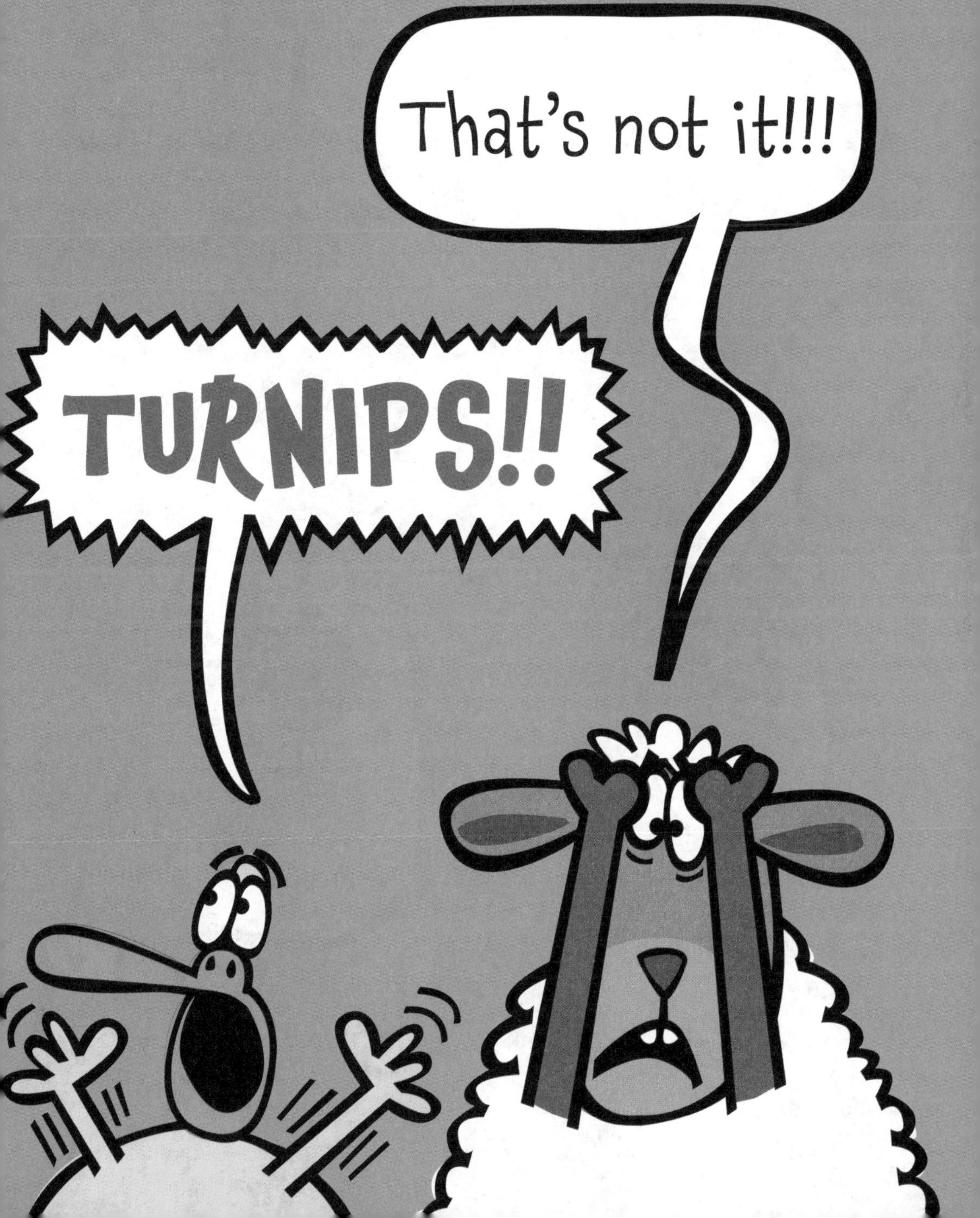
TURNIPS!!
That's not it!!!

OH! You make us **HAPPY** too, Sheep!!!

QUACK!

But, after **us**, what makes you **HAPPY**, Sheep?

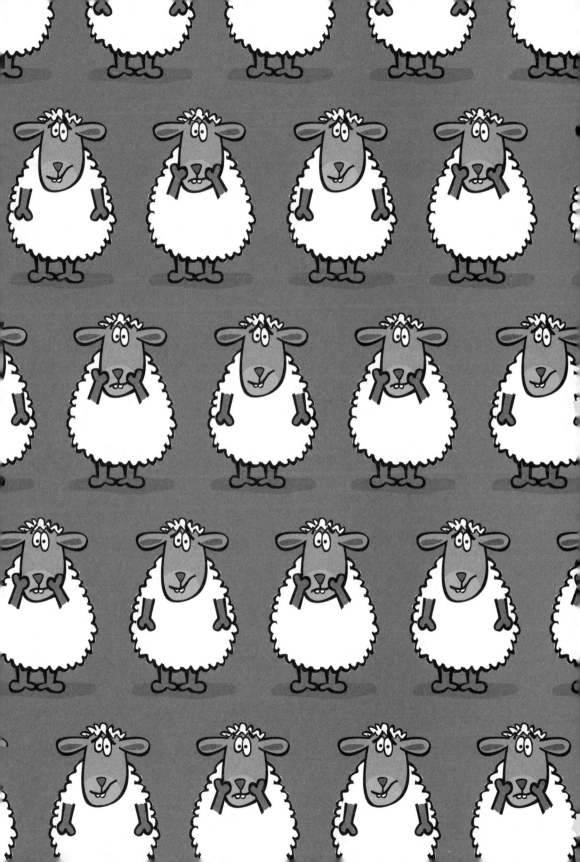